D0616834

14.-

5/10

Snack Attack

Snack Attack

Stephen Krensky

ILLUSTRATED BY
Stacy Curtis

Ready-to-Read
Aladdin
New York London Toronto Sydney

ALADDIN PAPERBACKS
An imprint of Simon & Schuster Children's Publishing Division
1230 Avenue of the Americas, New York, NY 10020
Text copyright © 2008 by Stephen Krensky
Illustrations copyright © 2008 by Stacy Curtis
READY-TO-READ, ALADDIN PAPERBACKS, and related logo are registered trademarks of
Simon & Schuster, Inc.
Designed by Sammy Yuen Jr.
The text of this book was set in Futura.
Manufactured in the United States of America
First Aladdin Paperbacks edition April 2008
2 4 6 8 10 9 7 5 3
Library of Congress Cataloging-in-Publication Data
Krensky, Stephen.
Snack attack / by Stephen Krensky ; illustrated by Stacy Curtis. — 1st Aladdin Paperbacks ed.
p. cm.
Summary: A cat in a shack tricks a rat with a snack.
ISBN-13: 978-1-4169-0238-6 (pbk)
ISBN-10: 1-4169-0238-4 (pbk)
ISBN-13: 978-1-4169-0239-3 (library)
ISBN-10: 1-4169-0239-2 (library)
[1. Cats—Fiction. 2. Rats—Fiction. 3. Stories in rhyme.] I. Curtis, Stacy, ill. II. Title.
PZ8.3.K869Sn 2008
[E]—dc22
2007019817

For Peter, who likes to snack —Stephen Krensky

For Colton —Stacy Curtis

A cat.

A cat and a snack.

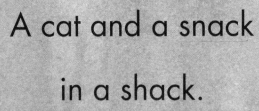

A cat and a snack

in a shack.

A rat.

A rat in a crack.

A rat in a crack in the shack.

"Ham and jam!" says the cat.

"What a snack! *Smack, Smack!*"

The rat has a plan.

The rat will attack the
cat for the snack.

Clash!

The cat has the rat.

The snack was a trap.

The cat has the rat in a sack.

The rat is mad.

But the cat is glad.

For the rat, that is that.

And the cat in the shack gets fat.